MEET ME AT THE COFFEE SHOP

POEMS OF LOVE AND LIFE

HERBERT MCCANTS

MEET ME AT THE COFFEE SHOP

Published by Southern Women Publishing

ISBN: 978-1-956653-03-8 (Paperback)

ISBN: 978-1-956653-04-5 (Hardcover)

Dedicated to my mother and father, Herbert McCants Jr. and Cathy M. Crawford.

INTRODUCTION

Since high school, I've been toying around with the idea of writing a book. Mostly centered around my poetry. First, as a sort of self-help guide to being a nerdy, confused, angry, know it all teenager with "introvertive" tendencies. Then as a way to be heard. Being sort of a known unknown amongst the popular and elitist of your school tends to quiet you. As I grew older and became over-exposed to life, I considered writing about some of the unbelievable situations that I've found myself in and trust me there have been some doozies! So, for years I've told myself that I would do both. A book of my poems and a book about my life...

Never mustering up the courage to do either.

At 48 years old, I am sitting in front of an 11-year-old Laptop (HP 2000 Notebook PC) pecking at the keys trying to find my voice again. I would like for you to sit with me and spend a little time getting to know me.

Hello, my name is Herbert McCants III... Welcome to my Insanity. :-)

To begin I must give you a "real talk" disclaimer...

I, like a lot of people, was foolish enough to participate in some of those online poetry contests a few years back. I certify that every poem and story that I've placed into this book is mine and original. I had to put that out there because like a lot of people, I'm sure, I won second and third place a couple of times.

So, my plan was to try and put my poems in chronological order from high school to current, but I got a headache sorting through everything. I did however begin to remember why most of them were written. So, I would like to hold a simple conversation with you. A real-life, honest account of the events, stories, and situations that helped create each piece. If you like this idea check YES__. If not, check NO__. Kidding of course. LOL.

LET'S GO!

1

I didn't get introduced to structured writing until my junior year in high school Creative Writing class. It turned out to be one of my favorite classes, second only to choir... Mrs. Myrna Pratt Kyser-Choir Teacher- R.I.P., I thank you and will love you always.

WE WERE TAUGHT an exercise called spring-boarding. Simply put, take some outside stimuli; music, a photo, a given word or phrase, and write whatever comes to mind. Here are a few...

Springboard: Antonin Dvorak- *Largo Symphony No.9.*

<u>His Name</u>

Majestically he sits. Watching all that he
    proclaims his own.
With a look above all that is royal yet deep in
    his heart, he is alone.
I sometimes call him "Your Highness"
    because in his world he is king.
But when he comes back to our world his is
    but only a dream.
In his kingdom, he is lord of his domain and
    all others run in retreat.
I sometimes call him "Your Royal Highness."
    You call him a beggar in the street.

.... Now I know that the Homeless person aspect was a reach. The music reminded me of a king's coronation from one of the dozens of 70s and 80s movies that I had watched around that time. I believe the movie *Excalibur* was my favorite back then. And maybe there was a picture of a homeless man or perhaps the subject was brought up in conversation, but I thought about a man pushing around his buggy/cart. All that he has resides inside that cart. Where he lays his head is his domain and he is king. Why can't he be regal in his own kingdom?

Springboard: A photo of two people holding hands.

Blessed Love

To live and love is truly rare.
To have someone who really cares.
To walk in the darkness no longer scared,
Simply because that person's there...
IS BLESSED
To hug and kiss the one you hold dear.
To be able to handle life because that
  person's near.
No matter the distance in your heart they're
  here,
And living without them is your only fear...
THAT'S LOVE

...IN ALL TRUTH, these were the fledgling steps of a hopeless romantic. I've heard that pain builds character and adversity reveals it. For a writer, pain and adversity give you motive and reason for expression, but time and growth give you the words. I had no clue who I was at that time. I had an idea. Quite possibly even dreamed about the man that I would become, but ultimately just a clueless kid searching for a voice.

Springboard: A discussion about life.

<u>Life</u>

The kiss of life is a thing of beauty. It brings
joy and happiness into this world.
The kiss of death can be beautiful as well as
sorrowful.
Although a loved one is lost the thought of
moving on to the heavenly hereafter
seems to make mourning as majestic as
praising.
But alas, the kiss of love, its appearance,
beautiful and timid.
As graceful as the face of Aphrodite.
But not really love... Life.

...OK, I said we were going to have honest dialogue, right?
Man, I was tripping hard with this one! LOL. It's all a
journey.

Springboard: *Piano Sonata No. 14* Ludwig van Beethoven.

Moonlight Sonata

I see a man mourning the death of his love.
He sits at his piano and begins to play a piece
    of music that the two of them started
    writing together.
As he plays, visions of their lives together
    begin passing before his eyes.
With every keystroke, He remembers that the
    love they had for one another was untar-
    nished. Suddenly he realizes that they
    didn't finish the piece.
So, he adds his musical farewell to the end of
    the song and their lives together.

Springboard: A picture of pandora and her box.

<u>Hope</u>

Evil, evil everywhere.
It surrounds me.
Trying to engulf me.
To swallow all that is the future.
They know that I am strong but against this
    much evil,
I don't know how long I can hold out.
They know that if they kill me, they
    have won.
Who am I?

Springboard: Riding in the back seat of my dad's brown on brown, 2 door, 1974 Buick Electra 225, staring out the window.

Clouds

Snow white mountain peaks.
Majestically high.
Forever at peace.
With heavenly tears and thundering sound,
Reaching for God but never touching ground.
They move and travel with the slightest
    breeze.
Losing their shape as they pass beyond the
    trees.
Now from white to orange as the sun begins
    to hide.
From beauty and peace to their darker side.
Come strong winds then rain.
We begin to ask why.
Now thunder next lightning,
God's fury from the sky.

Springboard: A commercial about the book *Dianetics* by L. Ron Hubbard.

Die-Who?

For thousands of years, man has pondered
    the meaning of life.
LIFE
Isn't that word in itself a contradiction?
To be born, by most standards, is the begin-
    ning of life but in keeping with life's
    cynical and hypocritical demeanor, death
    is the end of life's commitment to man.
WHAT IS THE MEANING OF LIFE?
The best definition by life's standards is that
    you are born then you die.
And somewhere along the way you're
    supposed to learn who you are, what you
    need, what matters most, extend your
    seed, and bring forth new life.
And inevitably die.
The period between birth and death can be
    happy and fulfilling or depressing and
    ever constant.
WHAT IS THE MEANING OF LIFE?
Unfortunately, the meaning differs for each
    individual.
I don't know what your life means to you and
    probably won't know what mine means to
    me until I've completed my mission.
Death is inevitable.

Boy! I thought I was as deep as the cosmos and twice as bright. I'm shaking my head and laughing at myself.

Truly it is so cool to be writing this for you to read. Some of these poems I haven't read in a gang of years. So, sitting here proofreading them has been a walk down memory lane of epic proportions for me. I hope that the simplicity of these writings hasn't deterred you from continuing this journey with me. After all, no story begins at its apex. As I grew, so did my writing. As I gained weight, so did my words. You'll see. There are a few more of these foundation-building poems. It gets better... I get better, I think. Take a break if you need to. Grab a cup of coffee, a glass of wine, a bottle of water and jump back in with me.

Springboard: Laying in the driveway of my mother's house
one night in Olive Branch, Mississippi.

A Childish Wish

Twinkle, twinkle little star.
How I wish that I was where you are.
Suspended over this troubled earth,
My dreams of the future are what you're
    worth.
I wish that I could shine as bright as you.
And paint the night sky the way you do.
And when there is no sunlight above
    my head
the cold concrete becomes my bed.
I lay and I stare at your beautiful light.
And your twinkle turns into my dreams at
    night.
But when the sun comes out and the sky has
    turned blue,
I will walk around this earth pretending
    I'm you.

THIS NEXT ONE IS A DOOZY. Here's the setup... I began talking to this girl at school junior year. She lived in Saint Mary's Home for orphaned children. Let's call her Clair. I don't know a Clair so calling her Clair instead of her real name shouldn't be an issue. We grew close very quickly. We would eat together at school when we could. Talk on the phone until her curfew. The home even gave her permission to go with me to the movies a couple of times. As forestated, hopeless romantic. Brought flowers to school the whole 9 yards.... Yeah, Clair cheated on me. Had sex with some random guy (I say random because I don't think I ever knew who he was), behind the cafeteria dumpster. Y'all know how the school grapevine works. I got a call much later that night from a friend telling me what she did. When I confronted her about it over the phone, she admitted to it. Said that I was really sweet, kind, and nice. Too nice. She said I never tried to strike. She was the first to dub me "Too Nice" and definitely not the last.

Springboard: Clair

<u>Blinded by Love</u>

Love can be a Ninja. A master of not being
    seen.
He deceives all those who trust him and have
    brought nations to their knees.
He comes in many shapes and colors like the
    chameleons of the earth.
The rich will shell out millions for him. The
    poor can't afford what he's worth.
He eludes all those who search for him. Like
    a fugitive on the loose.
And for those who don't expect him his grip
    is like that of a noose.
You never know when he'll hit you. Like
    Tyson running wild.
He's broken many happy homes and brought
    about many a child.
I don't know him as well as others. I've only
    met him once or twice.
But never in my life have I been blindsided by
    love the way I was last night.

OK, so honestly the next few poems aren't so much springboards as they are my true voice beginning to take shape. I met a girl from a different school who set my body on fire. Placing within me a sexual hunger that seemed almost lycanthrope. As you can imagine, being a teenage boy who couldn't seem to release enough energy during the day, couldn't punish enough people on the football field to be satisfied, and pumped more testosterone through my veins than blood, my appetite was ravenous! What I didn't count on... the thing that I couldn't fathom is that her thirst for touch was greater than mine. Y'all, know she cheated on me, right? In keeping with the honesty that I promised you at the beginning of this book, I hadn't found the "whore in me" yet. I was as loyal to romanticism as Romeo was to Juliet. But truthfully, I was more angry than heartbroken. The sting of betrayal twice in less than a year. Pain began to feel like a warm blanket in winter...

Questions

What is a rose if it does not bloom?
What is a bride without her groom?
What is a child without his toy?
What is life if there's no joy?
What is love if there's no hate?
What is a man without his mate?
What is the future if there's no past?
What is love if it will not last?

Inside Myself

If there was sunlight in my eyes the clouds
    have shut it out.
If there was joy inside my heart, there's none
    left to tell about.
I wish I could look inside my head and see
    what's going on.
I imagine that things would be upside down
    because it feels as though it's all wrong.
If there was happiness inside my soul, why
    won't it come out and show it?
If there was any love left inside myself, I
    really and truly don't know it.

<u>Alone</u>

Here I walk alone as I've done for so many
    years.
Stumbling through the dark trying to cope
    with all my fears.
Trying to piece together my broken heart
    while counting my ever-flowing tears.
Looking back into the past as my life
    disappears.

SHORTLY AFTER THAT fiasco and subsequent swearing off all women and that love was for suckers; I met the woman who would become my wife around 11 years later. But we're not there yet. We are still in high school. Our senior year, third semester and it was absolute love at first sight. She walked into church that Sunday, March 24, 1991, and I told one of my friends that I would marry her. She is going to be my wife! Oooh, the hopeless romantic was back!

My Muse: Jai

Fantastic Voyage

I want to take you on a trip to see what has to
    be seen.
A voyage that may take eternity.
A love imagined only in dreams.
You may never know how strong my love is.
You may never understand,
Why I place my heart, my soul, my love,
    comfortably in your hands.
The bond between us is forever and·can
    never be broken apart.
For I've made a place for you to lay here
    inside my heart.

The Sun

It rises in the east.
A symbol of our love.
Spreading its warmth and joy over my body.
The intense heat that emanates from its
    unknown interior symbolizes that my
    eternal thirst for your love cannot be
    quenched.
Yet, it is alone.
One of a kind.
No one really knows why it's there or what it
    really means but I do.
It means that my love for you has been
    around for millions of years and will be
    here for millions more to come.

WE CAN CALL this the end of Chapter One. I know that a lot of the poems so far are a bit elementary but that's kind of the point. Not to write a book of what I think are my best, most thought-provoking poems but to allow you to see the growth of me. How do I expect you to get to know me if I can't be honest about who I was as well as who I am? Isn't the foundation just as important as the building itself? Let's see what Chapter Two holds in store...

2

___

After graduation, my love and I went off to college. Her in Atlanta, Georgia, and me in Huntsville, Alabama. We went through typical growing issues being in different states and the strength of our connection was tested. I can promise you that there was a preponderance of poetry written during that time and afterward. Sadly, for this book and perhaps for the best mentally, the greater majority of those works have been lost to time and relocations.

Here are a few that made it this far...

Do You Feel Me?

There's a pain in my heart,
Like the pain in my mind,
Like the pain in my hands,
Like the pain in my behind,
Like the pain in my back,
Like the pain in my soul,
Like the pain in my fingers,
Like the pain in my toes,
Like the pain in my arms,
Like the pain in my legs,
The pain in my body makes me wish I was
    dead.
There's a pain in my head,
Like the pain in my heart,
And the pain is there because we've grown
    apart.

<u>Truth</u>

I'm sitting down to write this poem because I
     have nothing to do.
And thought of the person who means the
     most in my life and I automatically
     thought of you.
You are on my mind day and night.
My dreams are filled with your smile.
With one touch of your hand or a wink from
     your eyes
I feel like a nervous child.
The mere thought of us together, like boy,
     meets girl,
Makes me wonder if dreams do come true.
For in my dreams my only goal is to spend
     eternity with you.
You know how I feel about you.
You know that my feelings are strong.
But in this world of good and bad, there is
     something terribly wrong.
The reality of waking up.
Which means the end of my dreams.
I know that doesn't sound terrible, but
     nothing is as it seems.
For in my dreams, I have you, a picture-
     perfect romance.
But in reality, you belong to another which
     means I don't have a chance.
So, as you can see, I don't give up easily
     because I'm madly in love with you.
In fact, I'm a strong believer in the phrase
     "Your dreams really can come true."

Now is around the time that I started to understand that I could use my "powers" for good or evil. That there was an art to being single. This is also the time that I could lay absolutely no claim to being a saint. Loyal only to my baser need to dominate and control my surroundings. But the man that I was becoming was just an act. He was the bouncer at the door to the club. The real me never went anywhere. My ability to wallow inside my head and torture myself was ever-present.

<u>VCR</u>

Have you ever stopped to wonder why your
　　mind holds some things, releases others,
　　and places some on reserve?
Holding the things that you deem precious
　　and special.
Repeated recollection through proven points,
　　shared feelings, past regrets, and
　　emotional similarities.
Things that our heart has chosen to hold on
　　to, forever vivid, never released.
Memories spontaneously emerge that can
　　feel harmful or have no relevance in our
　　eyes.
A smell that reminds you of your high school
　　gym, which can turn to thinking of the
　　way people treated you.
Things that you thought were cast out, never
　　to be thought of again...
Not gone. On reserve.
Just run across something you haven't seen in
　　years and watch the movie which is your
　　life.
Press Rewind Then Play.

<u>One Man's Opinion</u>

The imagination is a powerful thing,
For destruction can come from one man's
    dreams.
Love is something no one can define.
Is it a feeling in your heart or an illusion of
    the mind?
Forgiveness is embedded in the heart of
    every man.
Put there necessarily to give people a second
    chance.
Curiosity can be dangerous.
And that is a fact.
If you don't believe me, just go and ask
    the cat.
Openness is a weakness we should take
    control of.
Often times it's betrayed by that thing called
    love.
Simplicity is man's downfall and our biggest
    regret.
Because the simpler you become the harder
    life gets.

Springboard: Listening to the rain.

Raindrop Serenade

I hear you calling.
Tapping at the windows of my soul.
Beating on the panes of my pain.
I feel you calling.
Moving me like the tree of life, which is my
    life, to and fro.
Swaying in your arms of gentle breezes.
I see you calling.
Lighting the dark skies of my pitiful
    existence.
Flashes of energy made up of past souls from
    past lives pleading with me to come home
    to peace.
I've heard your rage.
Pounding my soul and shaking the very
    ground upon which my foundation lies.
I've felt your rage.
Spinning and tossing debris at the structure
    that protects my whole existence.
The rain has a song to sing.
Can you hear it?
It's calling me...and you too.

READING these old poems has been so eye-opening to me. I may have been on an alternate planet when I wrote some of these, but I can still feel the emotion that was trying to be conveyed. Yes, I know it's because it's my writings. Lol.

LET ME ASK, how are you, reader? Look down to see if your coffee cup needs refilling. I just finished baking chocolate chip cookies for my 9-year-old. So, a pause may be necessary. No? Cool beans then let's continue...

HERE ARE a few more of my all-knowing, deeply philosophical, 20-something-year-old pearls of wisdom.

<u>Struggle</u>

Take two steps forward.
Now three steps back.
You strive to move ahead but there's some-
    thing you lack.
You show people you're happy but it's just
    an act.
Take two steps forward.
Now three steps back.
You must work hard all day just to make ends
    meet.
By the end of the week, you're tired and beat.
You go to the kitchen there's still nothing
    to eat.
You must work harder all day just to make
    ends meet.
You've got to choose a love who can provide
    comfort in your life.
Depending upon who's reading this, a
    husband, or a wife,
But you're tired of getting your heart broken
    and love cut like a knife.
Yet, you've got to find a love to provide
    comfort in your life.

<u>Joy</u>

At first, I had nothing but problems you see.
No money, no job, and no place to sleep.
Just bills upon bills that needed to be paid
And a stomach that hungered day after day.
But now I've got two jobs, a car of my own,
A one-bedroom apartment that I like to call
    home.
But problems keep rising which is strange
    to me.
My bed is untouched for I've no time to sleep.
My car is immobile. Which does me no good.
But I don't think the problem is under the
    hood.
I'm also in love which makes matters worse.
You'd think that'd be fine but too often I've
    been hurt.
I know I sound sad but really, I'm fine.
I'm writing because thoughts are clouding my
    mind.
I really am happy and why is this so?
Because Jesus Christ loves me and this I
    know.

AFTER LEAVING college I moved to Memphis, Tennessee. I adopted the nickname Devin, given to me by one of my closest friends to this day, Mr. Randy Rene Young. With the name also came a new personality. Devin wasn't the shy hopeless romantic that needed his feelings protected. He was the bad boy I never thought I could be. In fact, Devin is the nom de plume under which the rest of my poems were written. I grew in sort of the wrong direction. Learned a lot from the streets. Met friends who became family, and some became closer than that. If there is a word that means closer than family write me and let me know.

SAMUEL L. DIXON... Oh, the devilment we caused and came out of! LOL. The VIP Club, Club Memphis II, Black Cat, Club 380 Beale, Denim and Diamonds. Epic adventures! I was still in the process of learning who I was and trying to pave the way to who I was to become. But after three years in Memphis, it was Atlanta, Georgia that refined me. Smoothed out my rough edges and set me on my path to self-discovery.

<u>Revelation</u>

How did I get here?
Where am I going?
Who is my past?
Is my present worth knowing?
Is my future ahead of me,
Or has it passed me by?
Do I care to know the answers?
Does it even matter why?
Will I ever find happiness?
Will I ever feel her touch?
Will I continue to long for peace?
Or am I running out of luck?
Is it possible to grow old one day?
Or will I face an early death?
Will I live to see my grandkids?
Will I live through another breath?
Will I ever embrace loneliness?
Will I ever stop running from love?
Will I ever learn to do what's right?
Or keep sweeping the truth under the rug?
Will I ever understand my pains?
Or have they already taken hold?
Will I realize that I'm just like everyone else?
Or am I about to break the mold?
Is it possible for me to love myself?
Or have I dug an early grave?
Will I drown in questions of sorrow?
Or am I worthy enough to be saved?

IN ATLANTA my goals and intentions were simple - get a record deal, raise my newborn son, make lots of money, and be Mr. Charming covered in awesome sauce! He swings... He misses. One out of three isn't too bad.

ATL OFFERED a lot of financial opportunities, but it is a "who you know" kind of town. I rushed to the types of jobs that were easy to obtain, Security.

OH YEAH, did I fail to mention that I am a big boy? At that time, I was 6'4" tall and weighed in at about 235 lbs. Started working contracted security and then moved on to El Caracol Night Club. My personal life shattered during that time with my son's mom but that was Herbert's problem. Devin didn't miss a beat.

<u>Boys to Men</u>

If a man desires change, what is he trying to
    change from?
Bad to good?
Is desire without action enough to promote
    change,
From good to better?
How much desire must a man have in order
    to believe he can change?
Never considering the courage that it takes to
    make the effort to seek change.
How do you know when desire isn't enough?
When bad meets worse?
Has the thought of who you want to change
    into even set in?
Oh, I forgot...
The desire to change is enough to make man
    settle.
NOT!
How long will man settle for what he is and
    what he has before he realizes that desire
    alone is just as effective as driving across
    the country with no gas?
Is it within man's ability to let go of the idea
    that desiring to change will stop the worse
    from becoming unbearable?
I don't know... But I really desire the answers.

<u>Life</u>

To live and die a troubled man is hell within
    itself.
And poverty is a rich man doesn't know what
    to do with his wealth.
A burdened man is someone with an open
    ear to all.
And a prosperous man is sometimes blind.
    No appreciation for where he is until he
    falls.
A confused man seems to have everything
    but can't decide what to do with his life.
A blessed man deals with all these things and
    still gives his all to Christ.

The Future

Problems of this world got you down?
Smiling outside like the face of a clown?
Commonplace things begin to seem strange?
It's time to change!
Tired of life kicking you in the ass?
Can't move forward because of your past?
Waking up to a new day but tribulations stay
    the same?
It's time to change!
Giving your heart to those in need,
Only to find that they're filled with greed.
Giving love to the unworthy, now ain't that a
    shame?
It's time to change!
Giving joy to others when inside yourself
    there's sorrow?
Providing comfort to your friends when
    there's none left to borrow?
Just remember as long as there is hope for
    tomorrow...
There's time to change.

THERE WAS a true battle going on inside of me between '96 and '99. When I tell you that those 3 years in Atlanta, Georgia felt like 10 years if not longer. I experienced hurt, love, and loss on a scale unimagined at that point. I embraced the streets and all that that implies, all the while only allowing Herbert to come out from time to time so his muscles wouldn't develop atrophy. Devin needed Herbert's brain to keep him in check lest he be lost in his boldness. My writing helped so much but true to form I kept a distraction in my life. The woman I had been dealing with at the time had nightmares often. As long as I had known her, they plagued her. It took me a while, but I finally understood that there is no rest for the wicked!

Confused

She is Aphrodite.
Goddess of love,
Daughter of lies,
Sister of manipulation,
Granddaughter of fornication,
User of men's hearts,
Angel of death...
But she makes me happy.

<u>Nightmares</u>

For whom
Did the bells
Tell that hell
Is not within man's reach?
And why
Must man try
To fly so high
And have not yet learned to speak?
Is life
As true
Blue as you
Have tried to make me believe?
Or did you
Work hard
To get scarred and marred
And deserved what you received?
If you've
Heard a word
Of this absurd rhyme
You'd probably think I'm out of my head.
But nightly
Dreams
Of demons seem
A worse fate than being dead.

<u>The Walking Dead</u>

You dream about death, but you don't
    understand,
That sooner or later he greets every man.
Why live your life wishing you were gone?
Hoping and praying to be left alone.
Try seeing your life through different eyes.
Live it to the fullest.
You may be surprised.
Because if you walk around daily wishing
    death you could meet,
You should then realize that you're dead as
    we speak.

- Bernard of Clairvaux (c.1150). Hell is full of good wishes or desires.
- Ecclesiasticus 21:10... The way of sinners is made plain with stone but at the end, thereof is the pit of hell.
- Virgil's Aeneid (19BC) The descent to hell is easy.
- John Ray- A Collection of English Proverbs (1670) ... Hell is full of good meanings and wishes.
- Henry G. Bohn- A Handbook of Proverbs (1855) ... The road to hell is paved with good intentions.

.... OH, I know that you've heard that last one before. I referenced these to make a quick point. I am considering writing a second book of my life, exploits, and situations. If it's the good Lord's will that I, do I am going to go into truthful detail about some of the things that you've read in this book and more. That being said, I am not, nor have I ever been a saint. I have wronged as much as I have been wronged. There is a lot omitted in this book because this is not that kind of book. That comes later and I'll be honest then too. Pain is not one-sided, but my poems are. So that's all I can give you right now. A story, a glimpse into what made me write at that time. In my life and my relationships, I intended a lot of good. Some were intended to be temporary but the road to hell was traveled, nonetheless. Some I earned. Some I didn't.

<u>Luck Run Out</u>

You came to me,
You asked for what?
To set you free?
You're out of luck.

You kissed me there,
You asked for what?
For me to care?
You're out of luck.

You held my hand,
You asked for what?
To be your man?
You're out of luck.

You made love to me,
You asked for what?
Eternity?
You're out of luck.

You held my son,
You asked for what?
Another one?
You're out of luck.

You made me care,
You asked for what?
To always be there?
You're out of luck.

You touched my heart,
You asked for what?
Never grow apart?
I'm out of luck.

You rubbed my feet,
You asked for what?
To never leave?
I'm out of luck.

I kissed you there,
I asked for what?
For you to care?
I'm out of luck.

I held your hand,
I asked for what?
To be your man?
I'm out of luck.

I reached out to you,
I asked for what?
It doesn't matter anymore.
I'm all out of luck.

A Man's Hands

How does a man know that anger has rule
over his life?
His Hands.
When does a priest know that his faith is
lost?
When hands, once brought together in
prayer, now bonded to a whiskey glass...
His Hands.
When does a musician know that the concert
is over?
When hands, once practiced daily to bring
joy into his life now used to introduce an
artificial relief of a non-joyful life into his
veins...
His Hands.
When does a young man know that he has no
future?
When the same hands that once stayed up
late at night carving out his road to
college, now used to pass out vials of
petrified powder so that his family can
survive...
His Hands.
And when did I know that I was no longer a
gentleman?
When she took my son away from me,
.... And my hands began to tremble.

IN THE MIDST OF EVERYTHING, there was still love and affection to be found, had, cultivated, and lost. Happiness and sorrow. Scores of situations as well as a few situationships.

Then I met Somer.

<u>Rules to the Game</u>

Love your mate with all your love,
But not with all your soul
Because if all goes wrong,
And the love is gone,
Your heart is left so cold.
Love your mate with honesty and
    compassion,
Not with lies and distrust.
Because if you don't,
Absolutely won't,
The heart soon gives way to lust.
Love your mate for who they are,
Not who you think they could be.
And if you do,
I promise you,
Their love is yours eternally.

<u>Road Side Fantasy</u>

Her fingertip touch ignites the fuel that
    courses through my veins.
A gentle pressing of her lips turns my sanity
    insane.
A peak from her eyes sends waves of earth-
    quakes up my spine.
Her welcoming smile is that of an angel in my
    mind.
Her soft words in my ear are a pleasurable
    battle call to war.
Her presence gives me a sensation that I've
    never felt before.
The entanglement of our bodies give my
    heart reasons not to hide.
And the thought of making love to her gives
    me the will to stay alive.

In the Here After

We've known each other for many years
And though our pasts have been devoured by
    the Langoliers,
I miss the friend that I had in you.
Because no other friendship has been as true.
Although time has passed, and times have
    changed,
The sign on my heart still bares your name.
I pray that our souls may intertwine
Together as one in the great divine.
A love like no one has ever known.
And will grow centuries strong after our
    bodies have gone.

THERE WERE things that happened in my life around that time that screamed "It's time to go home." We've made it to April of 1999. Yep, I lived 10 years' worth of situations in three years. OVER-EXPOSED LIFESTYLE. I did not want to leave Atlanta, but I had to for safety and sanity's sake. I did not want to leave Somer but by this time she was not even mine to hold on to. We spoke before I left, and I got the opportunity to tell her how much I loved her. Necessity breeds sacrifice. I vowed to return to Atlanta in 6 months to a year. Until then it was back to Mobile, Alabama for me and the end of Chapter 2.

3

About three days ago I called my ex-wife and told her that I had started writing my book. She was very encouraging and expressed how proud she is of me for taking the step. She was my biggest literary fan back in the day and an emotional wordsmith in her own right. I asked her if I could use her nickname in this book. She said it would be fine. That being said, here's the deal. This woman set herself apart from everyone else by wearing my last name. So, there will be little detail surrounding a few of the poems that follow. Respect is due and respect will be given. Period.

APRIL of 1999 saw me moving back to Mobile, Alabama. Situations and circumstances concerning my life, my sanity, and my freedom dictated an abrupt departure from Atlanta. I moved back in with my dad and stepmom. Confused about what my next step needed to be, so I started going back to church. I had been a member of this church since the 11th grade. The pastor cousin to Jai, my high school sweetheart.

The assistant pastor was her stepdad, and her mom was a minister...

I FOUND out that she and her first husband were divorced. We secretly started dating again and it was great. Boy meets girl, boy loses girl, boy gets girl again!

Think I Won't

You ask me do I love,
So let me show you how.
If there was ever a time to prove it,
I think that you need it now.
Our lives may not be in conjunction
With the way, we think it should be.
But I would put out the flames of hell
If I thought, it would make you happy.
I would walk barefoot on the sun,
And steal the light of the moon.
I would turn the stars into diamonds
Just to see you swoon.
I would swim the deepest ocean depths
and find the rarest pearl.
I would shift the axis of the earth
So that I could rock your world.
I would lift you higher than eagles fly,
And place you on a cloud.
I would turn your raindrops into honey,
As it hits your chocolate ground.
I would fight off armies that would harm you,
With only my bare hands.
I would conquer the highest mountain peaks,
To prove myself your man.
All of these things and more,
I would shed blood to do,
Because I'm willing to change my whole
existence,
To prove my love for you.

IT WAS around this time when I was absolutely certain that I couldn't take another breath without calling Jai, my wife. I happened to hear a song one day that completely took my mental, *Love Me* by Collin Raye. As sad of a song as it is it spoke to the hopeless romantic locked just under the surface.

<u>Don't Give Up on Me</u>

Love abundant has been released,
Spirits now touched by light.
Malignant pains have now been ceased,
Wings of angels now taken flight.
That thing, once dark, I call my soul,
Is now the brightest candle in the sky.
My mind, so young, thought to be so old,
Found the fountain of youth in your eyes.
With touch of hand, you set ablaze,
That thing that was once put out.
You calm the rage of my eternal seas
With just one kiss of your mouth.
Lifted high upon love's breath,
When words escape your lips.
Sweet memories pulled from mental depths,
Past loves have now been eclipsed.
You shame the brightest starry night,
When your smile walks into a room.
And with a love that's mine through death or
    life,
You take away my gloom.
You make me see the good in man,
by changing my tarnished heart.
And I love you, eternal because I can.
Not even death will keep us apart...
"If You Get There Before I Do."

Springboard: The Mummy (Movie 1999).

<u>Anck-Su-Namun</u>

Many things get lost in life.
Some never to be found again.
And even though our grip is tight,
They still get lost in the end.
The things we seem to cherish most,
Are always the first to leave.
For the sweetest fruit is picked before,
The leaves fall off the trees.
And in our struggle to reclaim what was lost,
We very seldom find,
That it was easier looking back to faults,
Than facing the future blind.
You never get to possess the past,
Not even in your mind.
Because yesterday was not meant to last,
And tomorrow is close behind.
But there's one thing that I can say,
Will never slip my mind.
That is my love for you, my Lady.
It will stand the test of time.

...I Love You Jai

A ray of light shine through the clouds of past
    regrets.
An old life destined to start anew and
    nothing once was is set.
A single chance for contentment surpassed is
    what my heart has desired.
A flower whose beauty will ever last and a
    smile that will set me on fire.
A woman whose eyes can peer into my soul
    and love everything she sees.
And be by my side when I grow to love past
    eternity.
A Siren's voice to be my muse of emotions
    overflowing.
To help me plant the seeds of happiness and
    pray that they never stop growing.
Once upon a time, my perfect mate seemed
    so far away.
Then I bumped into you as if it were fate and
    my life was no longer grey.
You may not believe I'm describing you in
    this poem of perfect love.
But Jai give me time to prove it too.
Then there'll be no doubts because...

Springboard: Mother's Day

<u>My Wife</u>

A day set aside to honor thee.
Giving thanks to you from your family.
For all that you've done to keep us strong.
And the sacrifices made for us all.
We thank you from hearts, souls, and minds,
For being there for us when you didn't have
    time.
For knowing that things aren't the way they
    should be.
Yet you look past faults and love uncondi-
    tionally.
The strength of your heart transcends time
    itself.
And the measure of your love is greater than
    Egypt's wealth.
We love you and thank you for just being you,
Because no second thought's given to all
    you do.
We thank God for giving such a woman in
    our lives,
And I'm grateful and privileged to call you my
    wife.

Now as I forestated, I began to seek spiritual strength and understanding at church. Before moving back home I'd bounced around a few denominations trying to figure it out and fill the void that leaving my church home had left but found solace only in the streets. So being back home with the woman I'd longed for in a place that was familiar to my soul was a blessing. I called on Christ and He answered.

<u>Daily Jog</u>

Now and then from time to time,
I tend to run from my trouble.
Not physically just in my mind,
But it always makes it double.
The answers to questions elude me,
Or maybe I just pass them by,
Because I'm always running, running, and
    running.
If I could I'd probably fly.
I realize now that when I started running,
I left God behind.
Struggling to find answers,
That without Him I cannot find.
I guess I'll stop running now.
God's waiting on me about three years back.

Hydro-Changed

Aqua pleasure purified.
Born again because He died.
Cleansed with blood dripping from His side.
An old man passeth but the new man rise.
In His armor, no ill can touch.
He did what He did because He loves us so
    much.
The wages of sin He removed from us.
He is Grace, He is Mercy, He is Power, He is
    Love.

<u>Can You?</u>

Where is the soul located?

Is it within the body?

Racing through the highways and byways that carry liquid life from coast to coast of this continent called me.

Is it within the heart?

Providing a constant beat upon my breastbone to remind me of its existence.

Pumping life where life should not exist so that I may appreciate its importance.

Is it within the brain?

Sending electrical impulses like the strings of a puppet master through my fleshy mechanical being.

Controlling my every movement, my every breath.

Is it within the mind?

To me, the brain and the mind coincide in harmony yet on separate planes of reality.

The brain housing only that which the mind accepts.

Only what the mind allows.

Could it be hidden within the deepest dungeon in the farthest recesses of the mind,

Waiting for the key of death to release it from a prison of modern life, scientific theories, pseudo-religion, and day-to-day tribulations.

Where does the soul reside?

Can any person who has one answer the question?

Springboard: At home Bible study (each Wednesday night at a different person's home).

<u>The Gathering</u>

Gathered together in peace, Unheard!
No tension back building.
No violent words.
No drunken attitudes.
No herbal mindset.
No immature encounters.
No unlawful regrets.
No dark corner contracts.
No upstairs mistakes.
No bathroom outcries.
No parking lot dance dates.
No DJ shoutouts.
No roof is on fire.
No $10 admission for your dance floor
    desires.
Just me and my people trying to show each
    other the way.
My idea of heaven is this gathering every day.

<u>Lead Astray</u>

In a room where walls meet, Heaven and
    Earth,
Man struggles to define his Godly worth.
With bended knee and humble hands,
Searching for the truth in a calumny land.
His origins a mystery. His purpose unsure.
His knowledge a disease. His hope no cure.
From birth, man struggles to begin his life.
With age comes pain and stress and strife.
But with God comes patience and purpose
    learned.
Mysteries unfolded; knowledge earned.
Although answers exist for you to consume,
Only Heaven gives answers that won't lead to
    doom.

Now I meant what I said about not going into details about my marriage and I'm sorry if these poems don't fill in any holes for you. This is of course a book of my mind. A one-sided look at the things two people were dealing with. I was raised by gold. Bread to be diamonds. Struggled to be quartz and brought glass into our lives. The Bible says a double-minded man is unstable in all his ways. Maybe that's why so many of my poems contain questions. Hmmm.

Strive

As the winds of change blow to and fro,
And what once was is gone,
We tend to look back on yesterday,
Because we find that it's harder to move on.
It's our search to determine purpose in life,
That fuels our driving force.
Though we're anxious to get behind the
　　wheel,
We very seldom know the course.
The future is always in front of you,
Yet it seems too far to reach.
Like castle stones obstructing your path,
Transparent but too strong to breach.
So, a choice must be made within one's self,
To decide what course, he should take.
Shall we stand in awe of our accom-
　　plishments,
Or should we bang on the wall 'till it breaks?
Love seems to be the puzzle piece,
That can help our lives be defined.
And I love you dearly with all my heart,
But God's love is greater than mine.

First Impression, Last Thought

One word to you, "Hello."
In an instance, you wonder...
Who is this nigga trying to pull the trigger of
    your feminine sensibilities?
Aiming at the target of your womanhood.
Wondering, how did this scrub have the
    nerve to approach you.
One word from you, "Hi."
"How are you doing?" He says and there goes
    your mind...
No, he is not going to continue to irritate your
    bone and sinew, and nerves.
Trying to talk to you like he's really interested
    in the impact that life has on you.
Knowing he don't give a, Shhhhhhh, He
    'finna say something else.
"What is your name?"
"Why do you care? All you want is my legs in
    the air," you say to him lips closed.
You know that's all he wants.
Just another piece of society attempting to
    corrupt your motherly purity.
Future dramas flashing in your mind.
Soap opera bound to get rid of this kid you
    give him imagination...
"Shaniqua."
"I'm Devin, pleased to meet you."
So tired of this you smile real quick in an
    attempt to satisfy his futile curiosity.

Yeah, he may be cute but canine qualities
    service in your mind.
Prejudgment your only protection.
Never once thinking that this man could be a
    sheep in wolf's clothing. A man. A
    real Man.
...Naw, nope, none left, all dogs and he's prob-
    ably the biggest one of them all.
So, you decide to let this "come conquer me,"
    end up at your house, doing that doctor
    thang Just so I can come home one day to
    find you playing house with another
    mother go no farther.
You inhale anger and frustration, past pains
    and future regret raising four kids by
    yourself, Because this dog chose to play in
    the yard.
All feelings carried on air; you see.
Let's end this now!
"Pleased to meet you too," your words.
"This is my wife," his words.
Oh damn, your thoughts.

I WORKED for a couple of years as a court police officer during the first portion of my marriage. I spent a lot of time thinking about what our future held and how to prosper. Night shifts were the worst. 12 hours of an empty building, checking each floor, turning keys, drinking coffee, and watching security screens. I wrote a lot. I hate that so much of my writings have been lost to time. I spent a lot of time thinking about Somer. She introduced me to the writings of Dean Koontz when we were dating. He grew to be my favorite author. During that time, I noticed that my writing changed and was influenced by whatever book I was reading. Picking up new words (I love that part), maturing as it were. After failing the run portion, of the police academy, twice (wouldn't stop smoking cigarettes and was pleasantly plump) I took a job as a telemarketer. The voice that ruled a building was born! Lol. Still, I questioned a lot of things in my life. I also began to feel this new man that I had become weakening.

<u>Split Second</u>

Ticking away the hands of time.
Time to search for what I need to find.
To find a light in this darkness of mine,
Of mine you have. What I need takes time.

Hour upon minute my life has been drained.
Drained of life in Love's sweet name.
Now name me the man who desperately
    needs change,
And change love to in love without the soul
    being drained.

The fact that I love sends earthquakes
    through you.
You dream of steady ground, but dream is all
    you do.
So do nothing, stand still until the trimmers
    are through.
Through the mirror's cracked image
    wondering what happened to you.

But if all goes well my house will still stand.
My foundation concrete, the frame of a man.
My roof, God's power. My heat, His hands.
Looking through life's door wondering why I
    still stand.

Now I've seen my future through the eyes of
   the past.
Past loves who hated love because their love
   didn't last.
Last chance for redemption before problems
   amass.
Amass knowledge of one's self less your
   lonely love pass.

And now the hours have succumbed and at
   hand is time.
Time for life and true love at long last be
   defined.
Define memories so sweet that they fester in
   your mind.
Mindset? No regrets. Just moments in time.

<u>What About You?</u>

Build no pedestal in my name,
For the top may be too hard to reach.
And as I struggle to achieve in this limitless
　　life,
My wall of sanity is about to be breached.
Build no pedestals in my name,
Even if excellence I'm destined to see.
Because what you can reach with your
　　fingertips,
Could be a walk across the ocean for me.
Build no pedestals in my name,
For I haven't the balance to stand.
If I topple from the weight of expectation
In your eyes, I'm no longer a man.
Build no pedestals in my name,
I don't know if I can excel alone.
I know you've tried hard to put me on top.
But it's because you couldn't stand on
　　your own.

<u>Get A Clue</u>

Mine eyes have seen the glory of the simpler
    things in life.
To live for love when hope is lost and lose it
    once or twice.
It's hard to explain my feelings because I have
    no definition.
No way to let you know what's inside. No
    room for mistakes or redemption.
In my heart there lies a mystery whose clues
    are easy to discover.
But the answers will never be found by one
    who can't be my friend, just my lover.
I need a love that equals my own but there's a
    catch that I think you should know.
That if you love unbound, like the love you've
    found, my heart will never let you go.

<u>Random Thought</u>

Looking for something...
I already have.
Hoping and praying for something...
I reject every day.
Wishing I could be...
When I already am.
I know exactly where I'm going...
Even though I've lost my way.
I stumble in the darkness...
With a flashlight in my hand.
Searching for my manhood...
When I'm already a man.
Loving my life...
But hating the way I live.
Having more than I need...
But not enough to give.
Needing to be loved...
But I get that at home.
So why do I roam?

Soul Trip

A thousand-mile journey begins with the first
    step.
My journey began with the truth.
Will she still love me?
I look in her eyes and see a perfect love.
Will she still love my imperfections?
Traveling through miles and time and
    memories,
Can she still embrace forgiveness?
I've looked inside the places I've been.
Can she follow me backwards to get to the
    future?
Her smile warms my heart to the boiling
    point.
Will her touch cool my senses?
Her beauty radiates like the sun.
Will she bring an end to the darkness in my
    soul?
How far will I have to go to be with her?
Will she give me directions?
I'm willing to make the trip.
I've already packed my heart and I've gassed
    up my soul.
When I get there will she be waiting?
When I knock will she let me in?
If I tell her I love her, will she send me home?
Damn, that would be a long trip back the way
    I came.
But she's worth it, the trip.
I love you. Now what?

Obvious

A closer picture of the inward man can reveal
    a multitude of things.
From secret desires, long since forgotten,
To the destruction of your innermost dreams.
A photo finish of life no more remains in the
    scrapbook of our minds,
To terrorize the conscience with regret.
Or soothe the soul with one moment in time.
We often travel down roads grown over in
    search of the answers to ourselves.
And we place our minds in certain danger
    when we overlook the photos on the
    shelf.

THIS IS the end of Chapter 3. By this time, I've loved, I've lost, I've moved forward and thankfully I've learned. This book is begging to be transformed into a deeper look into my life. The memories that ebb and flow against the back of my eyes are the voices of banshees. Maybe a second book.

4

———

So, hello again. This was the era of true reinvention. My selfish phase. We've reach 2006-ish. I'm working as a bouncer part-time in the hottest clubs in the city during the absolute best time to club. The Krunk Era. Lil Scrappy, Lil Jon, Lil Boosie, Mr. Magic, Pastor Troy, the list is endless. So were the stupid choices that I was making. My bread-and-butter job Monday thru Friday plus overtime and the club life Thursday night thru Monday morning! And I had the nerve to exercise a cavalier lifestyle with chemical influences. And all that that implies!

LATER IN THAT YEAR, I started working security in a shoe store. Like I said, stupid choices. My bread and butter turned into crackers and mayonnaise. But a fat guy had to eat! A lot of time was spent sitting in front of a monitor.

I HAD time to marinate on the women I chose to associate with. Sad to say but there were a few overlapping situations in my life at that time but no vows of monogamy. So bad but not bad, right? Still, the romantic in me would come out from time to time. Not to impress anyone. Simply because that's who I am.

I Promise

Promises made with love's intent to brighten
    your futures path,
Are made void of substance as time grows old
    though the intent will always last.
And as words on clouds float from heart to
    mind expressing its sorrow unbound,
The intent struggles on to reach the heavens
    as its presence is seen raining down.
And though the day victorious intent will
    claim seems far from the reach of man,
I will struggle to show you the intent in me
    until the day that I can.

Just in My Head

I have a phobia, a fear, a terror that runs
    through my body as night falls.
Some people fear things that can be seen,
    heard, smelled, or touched.
I have a phobia.
The reality of terror for some people lies
    solely in the mind.
Places, flashbacks of events, nightmares if you
    will, asleep or awake.
They all take the same toll on the mind.
I have a phobia.
To further explain, some people fear spiders,
    some people fear dogs.
I have a phobia.
Some people have a fear of heights.
Some people have a fear of closed spaces.
I have a phobia.
Some people are terrified of their nightmares.
Some people are terrified of the smell of gas.
I have a phobia...
Of coming home at night and there is no one
    waiting for me.
Alone.
Alone-A-Phobia.

<u>Muse</u>

The relevance of time has faded away from
    the intense radiance of my joy.
The feeling like the embrace of Isis' passion is
    evoked by the sound of your voice.
And as emotions have changed with the
    passage of time as relationships often do,
Just remove the dust from the non-perishable
    mind and you'll find that I still love you.

Black Widow

Caught in her web but I'm stuck voluntarily.
Got loose once before. The situation started
　　scaring me.
Countless months of pain, she sucked the
　　love straight from the heart of me.
And even though I got away I can't stay
　　because she's a part of me.
Looking at the remains of those who came
　　along before me.
My sanity began to drain as my love
　　continues to be used poorly.
Maybe I'll quit struggling since I'm used to
　　being stuck.
There's nothing left of who I was. Might as
　　well let her eat me up.

IT's funny how society looks at men sometimes. That we are unfaithful, we lie, we break women's hearts, we are users...

LET me be one of the few who will tell you that yes, men can be dogs. From the standpoint of crapping in the yard and leaving it there to be stumbled upon. That being said... MEN ARE ROOKIES COMPARED TO WOMEN! At least some of the ones I've dated. Cats they are! Yeah, they crap in the yard too, but they cover it up and laugh at you when you unknowingly step in it with no clue. I have dealt with some pure beasts picked from hell's vegetable garden! I do tend to like them crazy, but the end result hurts. Glutton for punishment.

Cat Nap

Once upon a noon daydream,
I searched for a feeling that was true.
My soul was tired and my heart desired,
To be with someone like you.
But now that I've claimed you for myself,
And my heart has been placed at ease,
I opened my eyes and realized
I got just what I wished for,
A Dream.

<u>Interview</u>

If love were your job...
Would you get up early every morning to
     keep it?
Would you tell yourself how much you hated
     having it but that you couldn't leave it?
If love were your job, what would you do?
Would you stress to get there on time so that
     you won't get fired?
Would you break your back working every
     day for just a little return?
If love were your job...
Would you complain about the work that you
     do behind your boss' back?
Or would you tell everyone around you how
     hard your job is?
Or would you preach to everyone about how
     you don't get recognition for doing
     nothing.
If love were your job...
Would you come home happy or pissed off?

Catching the Wind

Why does happiness elude me?
I've found a four-leaf clover.
Where's happiness?
I've found a purple snowflake.
Where's happiness?
I've found love and love promised me
    happiness.
Where is it?
Is that possible, love without happiness?
Can happiness be found in the one place that
    I'm afraid to look?
If so, where is that?
Inside you say?
That's absurd.
I've looked inside myself and all I see is
    happiness waiting to change and love
    waiting to be used.

EVERY PERSON on the planet has their own love language. Mine is touch and attention. I give as well as I receive. In most of the relationships I've been in, in the past decade or so, I feel like I've been on the giving end way too much. In my past I took pride in the term "sex as a weapon" and there was an art form to the wars I started.

<u>Choices</u>

My mind said, "yes."
My heart said, "no."
My common sense said, "I shouldn't."
My body said, "so."
My intellect said, "it's wrong."
My bed said, "that's all right."
I'm trapped in one of life's conflicts.
The keyword is life.
What should I do now?

REAL TALK...

THERE ARE times when I miss the ability to fall in love. Love and me have not been the best of friends. Those who know me know that I am waiting on Wonder Woman and now so do you. That special woman who can tear down the barriers that hurt and betrayal have built. Love is not foreign to me but "In Love" eludes me fiercely. Working so much doesn't help either. No time to weed through people's BS in order to find out who they really are. Wonder Woman will lasso me with trust, beat me with honesty, and break my "In Love" free. At least that's my hope. It's what I'm waiting for.

<u>Uninhibited</u>

Pleasant moon of blood-stained hands,
Passion circles from traveled lands.
Melodies played by hellish bands,
Teasing the senses of a frantic man.
Easterly winds bring erotic tones,
Of mangled flesh and love pierced bones,
To entice the desires of lovers alone,
As ravenous appetites overtake their souls.
And as the death grip of pleasure consumes
    their minds,
Lust's morbid touch becomes easier to find.
Soon the minion of ecstasy devours their
    time.
For the gift of their flesh is the loss of their
    minds.

Springboard: The call of an insatiable appetite.

I Hurt

I understand,
That you want the man,
That sets your flesh ablaze.
Whose rough worked hands,
Is your skin's demand,
To rub all stress away.
And though the attraction is insane,
With our wordplay and games,
My response has to be one unliked.
I would love to leave you drained,
But I'm really in pain,
And have to say I can't tonight.

WE'VE REACHED a point where I need to issue a disclaimer...

THE FOLLOWING poems and stories will not be presented in a linear arrangement. As I read through my notes, some of the poems and stories left to add to this book have, as timelines go, already happened. I've had poems stashed in notebooks, folders, flash drives, old cell phones that were transferred to the new cell... So, to those who may see yourself in this book please don't take this next section the wrong way. This is not an admission of crossing relationships or situations. I've been doing my best to keep it all straight and some just got lost in the sauce. I am adding the poems and stories as they come up in my notes.

HERE WE GO.

5

I met a young lady at the Spanish club I was working at. She was there with her cousin who was a regular. Early to mid-20s, very pretty. She took a liking to me pretty quick and I to her. The conversations were pretty unbalanced though. She was as country as cold creek water and young to boot but hey, I'm an older guy holding the attention of a younger woman. I sunk into it. I drove almost 45 minutes each way to spend time with her. She was high each time I showed up and that was/is not my cup of tea. Twice she wanted to have sex and twice I told her no. Sober and coherent interactions only (I was maturing y'all).

ONE NIGHT she left her cell in my car and I promised to bring it to her the next day when I got off work. On the ride up to her place, her cell was ringing off the hook with messages. Yeah, I looked. She had been messaging a few guys in Mississippi and New Orleans about hooking up and how much it would cost, and they were trying to get in touch with her. Yep...Back Page! I was livid!

<u>Macintosh Mad</u>

I am in quite possibly the foulest, angriest,
    most hateful mood that I've felt in years.
I'm listening to gospel music; I've prayed that
    this be removed from me, and I can't
    shake it!
My core wants to cause pain.
To lash out in emotional turmoil at any in my
    path.
I'm scared because it feels so good.
It feels like life is pumping through my veins
    for the first time in years.
The destructive power that I'm feeling right
    now is as sweet to me as honey on my lips.
I'm venting, trying to recognize the alien that
    now inhabits me and deal with him
    myself.
I'm so angry that I'm twitching. I'm so glad I
    said no.

THERE ARE times when my anger gets the best of me. Hey, I'm only human. When I find myself struggling to hold together the thin fibers that keep me rooted and grounded it's usually because of one person. There will always be that one person who can flip switches in you seemingly with Jedi-like expertise and precision. Her...

<u>Mood Swings</u>

My mood is so over the top right now that
    when I look up, I see grass!
My anger burns like frigid death.
My emotions embrace the quagmire that
    coffins travel.
My mind... My mind is not mine to speak on.
It belongs to the pain that controls it.
I am He who suffers for others' delight.
He who struggles to maintain the appearance
    of humanity.
He who wishes to carve the flesh from the
    bones of my solace.
I am He, with outstretched hands, longing for
    rescue not wanting to be saved.
Beyond all this, I am blessed with burdens
    and struggles that strengthen me.
ME!
The man you truly don't know.

<u>Leo Life</u>

My mood right now...
An insidious quagmire of emotion
Devoid of recourse.
A conundrum

Shadows

Waiting on a moment that the sun will shine.
Leaving all of my darkness behind.
A new day, a new hope of life divine.
Ultimately waiting for an angelic sign.
But as light gives luster to past pains of mine,
Anger springs new wells in the fabric of time.
Darkening my pupils and leaving me blind.
But unearthing emotions of the worst kind.
Do I stand in my manhood?
Do I cower and hide?
Do I face my darkest shadows?
Do I run inside?
Or do I wait on the sunset to relieve my
    mind?
Because darkness brings safety as the pain
    subsides.

MY SECOND BOUNCING gig was at a club named Static City. I met a woman there who was soooooooooo fine! A beautiful person. Super real and untouchable. I was married and faithful at the time. (I told you. Jumping timeline).

YEARS later social media brought us in contact with one another. After a few conversations, she told me that she was attracted to me, way back then. And it completely blew my mind. I was clueless back then but now no longer married. So, we expounded on the idea. It was my first trip to Dallas, Texas.

<u>Snack Closet</u> (Insider)

I long for you like raindrops longing for
    the sea.
I crave you with ravenous hunger.
Wanting to dine on your desires.
And taste the sweetness of your smile.
But I need the approval of your eyes.
Looking at the image of possibilities
    within me.
Setting ablaze a forest of doubt in my mind
To make way for spring's renewal and
    emotional growth.
With just a glance you make me feel...
And that is good.

I TOOK a trip to Dallas a second time to meet a young woman that I'd met in a chat group. Believe it or not, the first and last of such encounters. She had/has such a genuine spirit about her that just seemed to brighten my thoughts. And as well as we clicked, as good as we felt together for months, I ended up shying away from her. My reasons were deep, not superficial as some might think, and definitely communicated to her. We've remained good friends but no more trips.

<u>Wondering</u>

I wish I was...
I longed for it...
Hungered at the thought of obtaining it...
Let it slip through my fingers...
Turned away from it...
Pushed it away...
But the desire to reside in it, perfectly, is
    raging.
Can I?
Am I even able to?
Do I deserve the chance...again?
Or am I doomed?

Springboard: A black and white photo of a woman's lips.

<u>Your Lips</u>

The palm of my right hand gently presses
against your cheek as my fingers softly
caress your ear on its way to the back of
your neck.
With a jealous need to join, my left-hand
mimics the right's flow.
I glance at the objects of my desire only to
obtain.
We are so close.
The rhythm of anticipation rises through soft
flesh to be felt upon my chest.
Staring through want and desire into your
once void vessel now being filled with
promise, you look longingly back at me
patient and excited.
My hands have become a home that has
blanketed your insecurities, made safe
your need to feel, and paved the way to
my fulfillment.
Soft and supple is my agenda.
You softly bite down on the corner of my
directed attention.
I slowly trace with my thumb as I move closer
intent on conquest.
Closer now.

The essence of our spirits mingle creating the
    breath of seduction.
Closer still.
Finally, we touch.
A universe of power and promise, energy, and
    passion...
A Kiss.
Such a simple thing.

Springboard: A Picture of a white door opening into a room of light.

<u>Breath</u>

I've suddenly realized that with being single
    comes silence.
My mind has begun to focus inward and
    reconnect with the man I've put away for
    safekeeping.
I've started writing poetry again.
I have replevin my desire for elocution (reac-
    quired my love for words and speech).
For so long I have buried who I am in a
    protective layer of distractions.
Responsibility became my mantra as my
    ability to relax waxed and waned.
But even if for the briefest moment here I am.
Me... Herbert
Saying hello to you all.
Most of you for the first time.

ONE NIGHT I was sitting at the bar of the Spanish club I worked at. My AI friend and little sister, Bartender Extraordinaire Trena Jones, had just made me one of her newest concoctions. A couple of shots of heaven mixed with relaxing sunshine. LOL.

I WAS SITTING, sipping and vibing to some awesome Bachata music when I noticed this young couple seated across from me. Mid to late 20s the both of them. Dude was pretty laid back and cool, but it was her eyes that caught my attention. The way she looked at him when he wasn't looking. Like every breath that he took was euphoric to her. She looked at him the way every man on the planet should desire to be looked at. I saw it. THAT IS WHAT IN LOVE LOOKS LIKE!

<u>Perception</u>

There is a look.
A look of awe.
Of all-encompassing emotion.
A look of excitement.
A silent language spoken to the soul.
A look of enchantment,
Erecting the foundations of present and
    future possibilities.
A look of longing,
Evoking the ancestors of wanted desires.
A look of fulfillment.
A moment of sheer wholeness.
Feeling complete.
A look of disbelief,
That someone could bring you to this height-
    ened state of awareness.
There is a look...
That comes with being in love.
I've seen it.
They look good together.

I WAS on Facebook one night scrolling through my feeds and came across a post from a friend named Angela. She posed the question, "What is your definition of beauty?" She is a deep thinker with a strong voice for uplifting the consciousness of the community and women in general. I loved our interactions. When I read the question and a lot of the comments, I remembered a photo that I'd seen somewhere. A Black woman with dark even-toned skin. A beautiful smile with a lovely shade of red lipstick. Gold and silver accents painted around her face as if to frame her image. Black and gold jewels in her hair pulled up in a bun. Purple, red, orange, green, and white tribal dress hanging off her neck and shoulders... and I thought to myself.

<u>Beautiful</u>

The definition of beauty
Is simple to define.
No, it's not the curve of her hips
Or the softness of her thighs.
Beauty is sometimes a simple glance
From far across the room.
A look that says "I know you're here
And I hope to meet you soon."
Oh, the smile of a woman embodies beauty.
The light that draws all men in.
A smile can speak to the heart of a man
and awaken his ancestors within.
The smell of her perfume,
The flick of her hair,
The touch of her lips,
Her skin laid bare.
This is the definition of beauty.
All or in part.
But her beauty means absolutely nothing
without God in her heart.

Springboard: A picture of a clock without hands and the numbers infinitely spiraling downward.

Wait A Minute

Time...
It's the only constant in the universe.
Time is an oxymoron of truth.
Invisible yet tangible.
Abundant but rare.
Touched by all yet remains pure and incor-
    ruptible.
Time gives meaning to every aspect of being.
It defines our choices and gives validity to our
    actions.
When time becomes selfish and begins to
    withdraw from someone it becomes more
    important.
Though more often than not the generosity
    of time creates a sense of nonchalantness
    in the hearts of mortal man.
We tend to forget that time is a gift given to
    us all,
To be used wisely.
It was our inheritance and from birth, we
    have access to an absurd amount of it.
And since this gift is ours to be used at will,
To be used at our leisure,
Used to give purpose to our lives,
Why do we have such a hard time sharing it
    with one another?
When do we realize that without time
    nothing can grow?

Nothing can strengthen.
Nothing has meaning.
When the recognition of times purity
    becomes prevalent
Only then will one realize how important it is
    to share with those you care about.
So, what's your problem?

JUST A HEADS UP, there will be several Facebook references with these next few... I'm just saying.

There was a young lady that I was following on the "Book." Absolutely gorgeous! Turns out that not only does she have an exceptionally intelligent brain but is a huge-hearted community activist. From time to time though she would share her hopes and her pains with us on the "Book." A gentle look into how human the incarnation of beauty can be, and she held my attention, from afar. I'm not that guy. We spoke several times, conversations about networking, a couple about personal issues and I followed her progress as she moved forward in life. Yes, she caught my eye but never acted on.

<u>Klassy</u>

I saw you smile not long ago
And I was instantly drawn in.
So innocent and bright it shone,
Made curious, the woman within.
I had an occasion to hear you speak,
With fervent wrapped intellect.
Your voice to me is a call to peace.
Speaking truths much worthy of respect.
I once got the chance to hear you laugh
And wished it was all my fault.
In that moment I...
...Noticed your eyes.
Incarnate beauty and delight.
Is it ok if I date your smile?
I'd like to get to know what it thinks.

<u>What-If</u>

What if I told you that you pique my interest?
What if I told you that I wanted to meet you?
Wanted to get to know the warmth that's
    expelled from your glance.
What if I told you that I see the pain behind
    your smile and want to know its origin?
What if I said honest and sincere words softly
    against your ear?
What if I could prove to you that passion
    exists without touch?
What if you briefly removed the barriers of
    past pains and allowed the spark of possi-
    bility to reignite the flames that once
    powered the forge in your heart?
What if we were meant to be?
What if you said yes to me?
What if?

OK, let's have a little fun with this next one...

<u>Xmas Rhyme</u>

'Twas the night before Christmas and all
    through the house,
I'm trying my best not to stuff all this food in
    my mouth.
No stockings in my house.
I don't get down like that.
I'm no crossdresser and I'm too damn fat.
My children are nestled all snug in my bed.
Watching The Lion King movie after being
    well fed.
I don't know what a kerchief is but getting
    ready for a nightcap.
And after I finish cooking, I'll lay down for a
    good nap.

ON YET ANOTHER post on the Book, my friend A.A. asked a question, if I'm not mistaken, about intimacy in relationships. I can't remember the exact question, but I do remember the words that the post birthed in me.

<u>Hero</u>

Heavy breathing
Erratic timing
Fingers gripping
Emotions climbing
Moans increasing
Strike gets faster
Deeper and deeper
I'm your master
Nails in my back
Pleasures death grip
Eyes turned white
Now biting your lip
Holding your breath
I feel you quivering
Goosebumps popping
Body shivering
"Oh my god"
gets released
Reaching for something
To bring you peace
Then when it's over
And you've calmed your head
I stand
Like Superman
At the foot of the bed.

AFTER GOING BACK and forth with A.A. and some of her friends on yet another post some random dude decided that he wanted to know who I was. I believe he posted a comment that wasn't quite palatable to the ladies, and he got irritated at their acceptance of my comment. So, when he openly asked A.A. "Who I was?" I answered...

<u>The Beginning</u>

Who I am is great.
What I do is awesome.
What I stand for is phenomenal.
The way I do it is professional.
The vibe I exude is masculine.
The hands that I yield are gentle.
The words that I speak are power.
I am a man.
I am a child of God.
I am Alpha.

...AND YET ANOTHER post from A.A. brought forth some mannish responses. I can't lie, I was feeling myself with this one.

Whispers

Gentle words spoken
Vibrate with every stroke and...
Warm emotions caress your secrets
As nails in flesh scream of release and...
Heavy breathing with rhythmic timing
Tells the story of orgasmic climbing.
Then "Cum for daddy" is whispered softly
As your muscles tremble and you doze off.

THERE WERE QUITE a few people that I've interacted with and responded to on social media. I can't remember who asked the question, but it was asked, "How is a relationship supposed to last when one person is ready to leave it at the first sign of trouble?" My reply...

Advice

Don't enter into a relationship with negative
> expectations.
Choose to be passionate about it because to
> me...
Passion lives in a place where the heart fears
> to leave.
Outside of passion is a place of loss and
> loneliness.
A good relationship has a fear of letting go,
A hunger for what's being fed.
If there is no fear and no hunger, is love in a
> relationship truly possible?
My advice is Passion.

THERE WAS a young lady in my Facebook news feed that posted about some things that she was dealing with and the pain and sorrow that it was placing in her. She'd always seemed so strong and confident in most of her posts. It was strange to read how vulnerable and timid her situation had made her. I began to think about women warriors in history. The Moors, the Amazonian women warriors of Carthage, Etc. I sent her 3 photos depicting these women and with each pic, I sent a passage which, read together, is one poem.

Springboard: Pictures of women warriors.

Fight On

> When the nights are dark, and winter is cold
> It's easy to lose your way.
> But hold fast to your heart
> And let warmth not depart
> For victory comes break of day.
> So, keep your head held high
> And shine in God's sight.
> Don't let trials define who you are.
> Only the strong can survive
> Is more than a line...
> Not muscles but character by far.

Springboard: A picture of a dead-looking tree with a beautiful green limb growing from it.

Pandora

I can give a man strength to free him from
    prison walls.
I can be a man's weakness to tear down his
    resolve.
I can be a woman's sunshine to brighten up
    her life.
I can be the author and source of all her
    strife.
I am the undisputed origin of this world's
    foundation.
I am the cornerstone used to build many a
    nation.
I am the most dangerous thing that you can
    give a man.
I am the most dangerous thing that you can
    take from his hands.
I am the eternal flame that can spark a
    revolution.
I am the anticipation of inevitable evolution.
Love may be man's strongest emotion.
Some may argue that it's fear.
But I am HOPE!
I encompass both.
So, love me and despair.

OK READERS, I am giving you all a lot of truth about myself
and my life. Let me ask you a question, have you ever felt so
overwhelmed by the weight of the world that you wanted to
cry? Maybe not even knowing why at first. Just a warm flood
overtaking you. I have and if you're truthful so have you.

Tears

Tonight, I almost cried...
My emotions could be felt rising.
Like the levels of time and struggle that are to
     be maintained and held back by cerebral
     levies showing no more respect for
     structure...
Rising.

Tonight, I almost cried...
I could feel my lungs fill up with the pres-
     sures of manhood and a lonely existence.
Drowning my heart in a sorrow most alien...
Breathing getting heavy.

Tonight, I almost cried...
Oh God, what is this?
My eyes have become weak!
An ocean of emotional pain can be felt
     crashing against the shores of my irises.
Turning bloodshot from digging into my soul
     to find the strength to repel the onslaught
     of memories that ebb and flow with the
     ferociousness of hurricane winds...
One drop.

Tonight, I almost cried...
Why should I give in?
I'm a man.
I will not allow this!
Should this continue then all that has been
    built within my being will come crashing
    down.
Forced to be made anew.
I will not allow this...
Exhaled.

Tonight, I almost cried...
I should've let it happen.
I would've found peace in release.
So now I fight on.

IN MY AGING I have developed a love for words. I'm also a bit of a movie buff. There are several actors and actresses that catch my ear when watching movies. John Malkovich, James Earl Jones, Kate Winslet, Bill Nigh, Eartha Kitt, and Hugo Weaving to name a few. I do so love to hear uncommonly used words with proper articulation. The speech by Hugo Weaving in V for Vendetta introducing himself is one of my favorite movie scenes. So, I found the bravery to write one similar...

Springboard: *V for Vendetta* (V's introduction speech).

Unrealistic

A proper presentation turns into...
Permission.
Permission turns postulatory.
Postulate gives way to proof.
Proof then becomes priority.
Priority leads to proposals.
Proposals lead to permanent perpetual
    passion purifying that person's position,
    positively, without poignant prattle.
Now pride's prejudice precludes a perfect
    purpose that's poised to peek and pene-
    trate the person possessing the pulchri-
    tude deemed provocative.

THERE IS a Starz original show called Spartacus. I really enjoyed watching that one. An artistic look at the historical accounts of a slave that led a revolt against the Roman empire around 73BC. The writers of that show are amazing. The wording, language, and enunciation of the script were just perfect to me. After I binge-watched all four seasons for a third time my mind was stuck in that mode of vocabulary. I started thinking about Auburn. You'll find out who she is a little later.

Springboard: *Spartacus* and Auburn

I Am Spartacus

My heart yet sits in shadows,
Marred and haunted by fleeting light.
A light so carried in my mind as to replace
    the shining of your smile taken so far
    from me.
Were I the master of time I would not have
    it so.
I would that the warmth of your breath yet
    caress my lips.
That a dance of flesh upon flesh become our
    mantra.
And yet, this burden of love I carry deprived
    of its return,
As if a child sickened with malnourishment.
That thing within my chest which pumps life
    to my body does so absent of meaning.
For nothing holds such sway over the reason
    for life than to be loved by one such
    as you.
The world shall greet me each passing
    moment as a ghost yet living.
For without love my breath holds no
    meaning.
Without you, the word carries no weight.

Springboard: A drawing of a black woman running through the woods carrying a child in each hand, two running beside her and one on her back.

The Black Woman

Her feet have walked through tribulations,
Over paths not meant to be tread.
Through ancient miles of hardship,
She has cried, hungered, and bled.
On her back, she has carried a nation.
The scars of which have sparked freedom's
    fire.
The perfect curves of her pain speak volumes
Loud enough to invoke conflict or desire.
Her seductive shoulders carry our future,
As she wades through the swamp and the
    marsh.
For when a child is carried on shoulders
They never notice that this world is so harsh.
Her mouth speaks with the wisdom of
    ancestors.
An eye's glance has the power to create.
The slightest touch of her hand has built
    cities.
A solemn teardrop has brought nations a
    menacing fate.
But her melanin is the jewel of the universe...

THERE ARE times when people can bring me to the brink of stepping out of character. Such a funny term. As if the person that I present to the world is a fictional person put on over the true me to pass as normal in this stage show called life...

I DIGRESSED, sorry.

SOME PEOPLE just aren't happy unless they bring anger and negativity out of you. I enjoy the power behind being in control of myself. To be able to stand in the face of adversity and give it sharp, edgy, and sarcastic responses, love it! The few times that I have lost it though are scary to me. I know in my heart what I would and would not do but it is in those times that I'm not actually myself. I am the anger that was sought. So, this next poem is where my mind went during one of those moments. And yes, it was that ONE person again. I am really considering that second book. You all could use more context about these people...and me.

Springboard: A photo of Batman in the grey Bat-suit, black emblem.

<u>Alter Ego</u>

Losing control, the illusion anyway, is not an
    option.
Allowing anger to cloud my judgment is not
    an option.
Assessing a situation through the eyes of pain
    and confusion is not an option.
So, I sit.
I watch.
I listen.
I wait.
Rationale be my comfort.
Logic is my friend.
I sit through days of honest dialect and take
    action in the darkest truths.
I am the night.
Seated on the throne of turmoil and tribu-
    lations.
There I shine.
There I rule.
There I'm tired of being.
And yet, who can take up my mantle?
To find familiarity in isolation?
Who else is willing to embrace the warm
    dark blanket of loneliness?
My reflection only answers.
I Am Batman!

Springboard: Me... Self-Assessment

<u>Planet Herb</u>

The tectonic plates in my world exist to create
    a new Pangea.
A new solid ground.
A new me.
Out of the Vulcan ash and earthquake rubble,
    a new continent of consciousness will be
    born.
Washed and cleansed by the tidal waves of
    the past.
My life.
My Earth.
A new beginning.
Good morning.
I overlooked the fact that this type of
    occurrence,
Mass extinction event,
Most lives would be snuffed out by such
    dramatic change.
But the strong in me, those people meant by
    God to stay,
Would repopulate my consciousness.
Revitalizing the spirit of the new me.
Earth-Herb

OVERALL, I can say that I've led a truly overexposed and cavalier lifestyle. In our youth, the new and exciting is never dangerous. I remember as a boy I would spend weekends and summers at my grandmother's house in the country. It was nothing for my cousins and I to be running around through the woods. Sometimes bare feet, shorts, T-shirts, and not a care in the world. I'm up in age now where I wouldn't dare to live like that. My past, I've lived it. I thoroughly enjoyed it. But 20/20 hindsight shows me the dangers I traversed.

I WANT TO BE MARRIED, still.

MY HEART IS OPEN, still. The things that I have experienced have not diminished the hopeless romantic in me. I am still Herbert.

Springboard: A picture of a man and woman in an embrace, carved into a living tree trunk.

Tree of Knowledge

In the truest sense of being
You were made to be with me.
Our love rooted in earthly desire.
Our passion sung by the gentlest breeze.
I am in the likeness of Adam.
First to ask God to be made whole.
From my body you were hued.
Destined to never be alone.
Our foundation is in God
As He nourishes our lives,
We shall grow,
Bear fruit,
Never separate.
My wife.

Springboard: A golden hand clock on a black background with stacks of gold coins coinciding with each number.

<u>Tick Tock</u>

10...

I pray to the Father on my knees with bowed head.

9...

That my family be protected from doom and dread.

8...

That on the morrow I see blessings in the breath I take.

7...

That He procures my soul should I not wake.

6...

That my children be blessed and know that I have tried.

5...

That the distance between us shall not rule over our lives.

4...

That He guides my Princes into Kings so that they may stand.

3...

That my Princesses mature into Queens with humble ruling hands.

2...

I pray for wisdom and knowledge and the power to do what's right.

1...

I pray for the strength to stand, come what may and all in the name of Jesus Christ.

I WAS SITTING down thinking about all of the relationships and situationships I'd been in. Women that I knew loved me and for whatever reason just didn't work out. I remember asking myself, "What's wrong with me? What is this hole in me that I just can't seem to fill? How is it possible to be happy and empty at the same time?"

Batteries Not Included

I think I'm broken.
My heart's not working right.
Incapable of falling in love again.
There are pieces missing out of my box.
My instructions tell of the tools needed to fix
    me, but it seems none can be found.
I've been open to quite a few relationships,
And the package clearly states, "some
    assembly required."
So why am I not put together?
Why am I not yet whole?
Why isn't anyone taking the time to read my
    instructions?
They are simple and plain as could be,
I know!
I'm still under the manufacturer's warranty.
So, I searched...
God being my origin, I returned to you
    broken.
I return to you, not whole.
All I want is to serve the purpose I was
    created for.
God said, "The power that you need, I'm not
    in you properly."

I SPOKE a while ago about a woman named Auburn. Again, that's not her real name but an insider representation should she ever read this book. She's been looming in the background of my life for years. A kind of silent crush. Now down through the years, I've told her how I felt about her and at the same time questioned why I do. She's done nothing to earn my love but for some reason, I've felt a strong desire to give it to her. I think she has me cemented in the friend zone plus the pains and caution lessons of my past won't let me fully pursue her. So, I'm just stuck feeling. Here are a few "Odes to" about Auburn.

<u>Dreamer</u>

So often I've wanted to call you
And ask you about your day.
To talk about the things I've been through,
To hear you say, "It's ok."
To share with you things that are on my mind
And pray that you give me yours.
To listen to the matters of your heart
And hang on your every word.
To imagine the curve of your lips
As you laugh at something silly I've said.
To be a listening ear when things go wrong
And have my words tuck you into bed.
To reach into the prison of my soul
And release myself to you.
To pour out words tainted with desire
Knowing you thirst to hear them too.
I often dream that this could happen,
Be it day or at night.
Thoughts of my future and there you stand
And for the moment all the world seems
    right.
But reality comes knocking and once again
I attempt to let you go.
Because you only look at me as a distant
    friend
So, no need to even call your phone.

<u>Awe</u>

Why can't the sound of my voice be greater
    than your silence?
I had hoped that audible thoughts and high
    decibel emotions would reverberate
    throughout your soul,
But to no avail.
Taciturnity abounds in place of the hopeful
    song I long for.
With outstretched arms, I crave for your
    whispered rejoinder...
And finally, "Awe good night, friend."

<u>Curacao</u>

Bad rum. Bad!
I'm sitting here in Orange Beach on the 7th-
　　floor balcony of my room,
Listening to the waves crash against the
　　shores.
Under the light of the full moon thinking
　　about impossibilities.
She, the imagined angel sent to ward off
　　loneliness.
She, the comforting warmth meant to stave
　　off frigid solidarity.
She, whose open arms present themselves
　　untouchable.
She, whose smile and form remain elusive.
*******Takes another sip*******
She has a name.
I know her well.
Her name is Fictitious.
Damn Rum!

Springboard: Picture of the Milky Way

<u>The Big Bang</u>

I have a desire to converse with you, Creation.
To build from dust a bond of eternal lasting.
To plant the seed of forever into fertile possi-
    bilities.
Efforts exacted towards love's fruition are met
    gladly by the vision of you.
I want to reap the rewards of the universe's
    promise.
To be made anew.
As if a star being born in the darkness of
    space.
Three words from your lips have the power to
    bring life where life does not exist.
The creation of one from two.
To be made whole.
To be loved.

Magnetic

Her tears weaken my resolve.
Her pain tears down my walls.
Her love, so much of what I want.
Want?
An illusion.
Need?
Reality.
Hurt,
Sorrow,
Me,
She.

So now we have reached the end of this chapter. I'm telling y'all, reading over some of these poems, remembering the context and situations that brought them about, has been real interesting. There are people from my life that have been left out thus far. Mainly because I went through long periods of not writing. There were times I felt like I completely lost the love for and the ability to write. So, to those of you looking for your influence in this book please know that it's here.

6

———

We have reached some of my more recent works. I also plan to add in some "mood" writings. Mood writings are just some thoughts and feeling that pop up in my mind. Sometimes due to things I've read of other people, concerns that I may have but more often than not they are due to insomnia scrambling my brain. I hope that you enjoy the ride.

Springboard: A Facebook crush who politely shut me down.

First and Twelve

I said I wanted to get to know you better.
You said I know enough.
I said I wanted to smooth the lines
    between us.
You said that you like it rough.
I told you I wanted to be closer.
You said the distance was just fine.
I made a play to command your attention
And you told me to give you some time.
I told you I wanted to be the cause of your
    smile
And you thought that I was running game.
I told you your beauty makes the universe
    insecure
And you curved me back in my lane.
Now embracing the epiphany of a futile
    campaign
And exhausted efforts to change our
    situation,
I move and I stand,
The proverbial man,
Who accepts that there is no remediation.

Springboard: I asked God to remove a woman from my life
if she wasn't meant for me and He answered, epically!

The First Day

In the beginning of our relationship, our
    world was without form and was engulfed
    in darkness.
Void of substance.
And the Spirit of God was invited to move
    upon the face of our waters.
And He saw that something was missing.
So, He said, "Let there be light."
Truth was born and our days were numbered.
The darkness hid your transgressions.
The light revealed them.
I thank Almighty God for the day
Because the night alone would've killed my
    heart.

So, one day I'm on a Facebook Messenger call with a friend and she asked me to call her on Instagram. I told her that I didn't have an IG account (really thinking that I didn't). She sent me a screenshot of my profile page. I had opened an account like 4 years prior and thought that I deleted it. Go figure. We talked for a bit and when our conversation was over, I decided to play around on my IG account for a while. I got a message notification. Four words... "What's up old man"?

FOR A BRIEF MOMENT, I struggled to figure out who this person was. The last name was foreign to me but that first name, Somer, now I know that name but who could be contacting me that spells their name like she does? People when I tell you that my brain did not want to put two and two together but when it finally did, after what seemed like 5 or 6 minutes of deep thought but was actually a few seconds, I jumped up and down like a little kid outside of a toy store! Somer, my Southern Cheyenne, my never forgotten piece of my heart, stopped my world from spinning with four words. ROAD TRIP!!

Happenstance

You finding me was too good to be true.
Looking for one another in a fog of trial and
     error.
Your smile to me is light in my darkness.
Your touch is warmth in the frigid depths of
     my loneliness.
You are the ember that reminds me of the fire
     that I used to hold.
And that feels good.

SOMER AND I have always shared a love for reading. She turned me on to Dean Koontz back when I lived in Atlanta. To date, he is still my favorite author. She and I were talking about a few of his short stories, and I got an idea to try to impress her.

Springboard: Paying homage to Dean Koontz.

<u>Books</u>

> The Intensity of my current emotions has
>   kindled a Cold Fire in a heart that was
>   Icebound.
> Leading me down Strange Highways.
> How Odd Thomas must have felt when he
>   declared to Fear Nothing.
> Only to break at the thought of being the
>   Sole Survivor of What the Night Knows.
> My love becomes Shadow Fires as The
>   Darkest Evening of the Year approaches.
> The Winter Moon exposes The Eyes of Dark-
>   ness as The Key to Midnight is lost.
> Your Heart Belongs to Me echoes throughout
>   The Taking of My Mind.
> Pain speaks loudly from its Hideaway.
> In an attempt to restore my sanity and Seize
>   the Night my heart calls forth Dragon
>   Tears as Lightning descends before The
>   Watchers.
> Phantoms of the past, I love you with a heart
>   that's not mine.
> It's yours.

Springboard: A picture of a castle's moated entrance with a bridge and raised gate.

<u>Checkmate</u>

THERE IS an onslaught of uncertainty crashing against the keep of my being.

A siege set forth by life's army of anguish and lessons.

Through patience and time, I've fortified my stronghold.

None may enter against my will and my walls shall not be breached.

...and yet, an enemy lies in the midst,

Weakening my defenses.

Laying bare the soft points of entry to which life seeks to use to its advantage.

Because of who has betrayed me I am no longer safe.

The secrets of the keep have been revealed.

All of my doings have been undone by an enemy within.

I am exposed.

Inviting the patrons of a carrion festival to comfortable surroundings.

For all my strengths, all my struggles, all of my sacrifice, building, and resolve, my emotions betrayed me.

My walls have been breached.

My stronghold, razed to the ground.

My heart, my love, my weakness.

You have killed me.

The king meant to protect you now needs protection.

<u>What's Up Old Man</u>

My heart has betrayed my reasoning.
Planting seeds of want and desire into fertile
    ground.
And the promise of a bountiful harvest is a
    sad occasion...
Because it takes me farther away from the
    person I've been struggling to become.
They say that admittance is the first step to
    change but I know the direction that my
    choices are leading in and still I lack the
    strength to turn back my course.

<u>Apologies</u>

There is an idea of you that I've carried in my
　　mind for twenty-one years.
There are memories of us that have taken
　　root in my heart and invaded my sanity.
There are traces of your touch, your smell,
　　your taste, your smile, your glow inhab-
　　iting the core of me.
I love you is too simple a term.
Reasoning aside...
I AM YOURS.
...and yes, I love you.

THE FOLLOWING writings will be my "mood" works. Quite a few little thoughts and feelings jotted down at different times. Honestly, though, the majority of these were insomnia-driven. I've thought about combining some of them in an attempt to make longer poems, but the flow doesn't quite work for me. The original points seem better, short poem or not. You be the judge...

******MY MOOD******

<u>Serenity</u>

I FEEL like a rock on the shore.
   My issues ebb and flow but are always there.
   One day my rough edges will be smooth but until then
The crashing sound of my tribulations calms those
around me.

<u>Insomnia</u>

I'm having trouble feeling like me.
Not understanding why my core's absence
    has become my reality.
Loneliness presents himself as my true friend
    as I am greeted by a thousand smiles and
    a few I love yous.
I question the man in the mirror but to no
    avail.
He cares about me as much as you do.
But do not fret. I wear those shoes well.

Greetings

A casual hello can spring forth an inviting
    smile,
Like the creation of the universe with lips.
Thoughts of wonder and desire given permis-
    sion to run wild,
As my mind's touch longs for your hips.
Hours of pleasure take hold and consume all
    thought,
In the seconds that it took for us to speak.
I turn away with a blush,
Thoughts unacted upon are hushed,
Yet the look in your eyes leaves me weak.

Springboard: A picture of a mountain cliff.

<u>Rock</u>

Who's there to hold the hand of the hand
    that holds up the world?
Who's willing to give a shoulder to the
    shoulder that bares foreign weight?
Which of you has an ear for the lips of ears
    that readily listen to all issues in earnest?
Not many.
Everyone's not built the same.

Springboard: A picture of a couple dancing not looking at
each other.

Bachata

When I dream...
I can see music.
When I dream...
I can hear your smile.
When I dream...
I can taste your laughter.
When I dream...
My soul knows you but please look at me
    before I wake up.

Springboard: A picture of a live oak tree with octopus-like branches.

Immortal

Imagine an oak tree,
Old and wise.
Once seed to sapling,
A master of time.
Immovable and proud.
Rooted deep and strong.
Connected to this world,
But ultimately alone.
Now open your understanding,
Relax in the shadow of me.
Wind rustling echoes of the past.
Sit with me, this old oak tree.

<u>Late Night Mood</u>

I am really in the mood to host a conclave of
    seductive colloquy.
A difficult undertaking in seclusion.
And yet the desire remains.

<u>The Graduate</u>

There are times in life where silence is louder
    than a scream.
When indecisiveness chooses an outcome.
When loving someone causes pain.
When following your heart leaves you lost.
Those times in life are teachers.
Learn from them or end up in summer
    school.

Springboard: A picture of a swordsman standing in a sunrise with a gun on his hip.

<u>Ronin</u>

I am a knight with no quest.
A warrior with no cause.
A patriot with no country.
A nobleman with no queen.
Lord of no lands.
A fighter poised for a battle that never comes.
I am a man in isolation.
Make no mistake.

Springboard: A photo of piano keys on fire.

Concerto

Every love song I hear, especially the ones
    with deep-rooted lyrics,
Have me thinking about possibilities.
Tangible circumstances that are right in front
    of me,
But just out of reach.
So, I give in to the melodies.
Surrender to the untouched passion of words.
And when the music ends,
When the quivering that's caused by
    thoughts of love's potential have subsided,
I see your face.

Double Entendre

Why do so many people hate change?
I've never had a problem choosing between a
    dollar bill and four quarters.
Yet people reject change.
Whether you choose change or not...
Don't you still get what you want?
Marinate on it.

<u>Contradictory</u>

I've often heard that opposites attract.
It's a matter of fact in science.
But when dealing with emotions,
It's a ludicrous notion,
More so when the heart is in compliance.
Positive and negative,
Yin and Yang,
The ebb and flow of energy.
All phrases defined,
In a universal divide.
The hope of finding glorious synergy.
But truth in the left hand
Is not always true for the right
In whole or even in part.
A darkened heart has no place in your light.
The magnetic pull of some people is stronger.

Springboard: A man sitting on a bench alone at night in front of a mountain and a full moon.

Herbert

As night proclaims its hallowed dominion,
I sit and long for love's light.
For in dark isolation I dwell,
Absent warmth, Its own hell,
With no redemption to correct my plight.

No Title Just a Mood

I'm feeling poetic right now.
I have a wellspring of words overflowing into
    my consciousness.
Billowing over my soul's shores.
Bringing with it an emotional surge of vivid
    memories and reality's certainties.
I feel...
I am alive with words strong enough to stop
    the beating of hearts.
I long...
I wish with all my being to bestow the verbal
    essence of this man to the waiting ears of
    she who is made by God to receive me in
    earnest.
I am...
I am the book of literary soul.
I am my words.
Take from me what you will and know me.

Springboard: Lying in bed feeling some type of way.

> I feel like being romantic.
> I am in the mood to stimulate the cerebral
>   erogenous zones,
> Creating an explosion of orgasmic energy in
>   the neocortex
> Without one touch of my hands.
> Only the caress of words.
> Are you ready?

<u>Genesis 2:22-23</u>

Before sleep overtakes me marinate on this...
When you're looking for love what exactly
    are you looking for?
That feeling of oneness with another?
The caress of another's passion piercing into
    your core?
That long hungered need to link minds with
    like minds?
I know what I'm looking for...
My Rib.

<u>Random Thoughts...</u>

I want...
But I can't tell you that.
I desire...
But you aren't ready.
I need...
But I can't find you.
I thirst...
But there is no one to provide.

<u>Como Va Su Dia?</u>

Some days are stranger than others.
There are days when my thoughts are all over
 the place.
Days when reality is just beyond my
 fingertips.
Days when I see beyond the veil of life's
 truths.
There are some days when every question
 has a rational answer.
These are the days when I question my
 sanity.
Tackling the insane moments usually keep
 me sane.

<u>Choice</u>

I understand expression with the use of
    emotional vernacular.
Feelings being painted with syllables and
    sentence structures.
But to everything in life, there is a core.
A foundation of meaning on which to stand.
To be heard in the heavens that what I feel
    has strength, meaning, and purpose.
I hear your emotions and I feel your sound.
And I bow my head humbly, taking my place
    as your pleasure and pain.

Springboard: Picture of a man in a suit of armor, on a horse with a javelin.

<u>The Quest</u>

While you're sitting back waiting for your
　　knight in shining armor remember this.
Old dude in the dull, beat-up, scratched-up,
　　dented, tarnished armor has been
　　through more.
Learned More.
Fought for what he believes in.
Understands more.
Has more patience.
Keep chasing that brand-new armor.
After a while, you'll understand what I'm
　　saying.
Your gear will be a little scared up as well by
　　then. IJS.

Unity

There are times in life,
More often than not,
When joy seems to be an illusion.
And although we desperately long for love,
Once received we deem it an intrusion.
Loneliness seems to be the element that
        drives us to inclusion.
But many times,
We tend to find,
That person causes confusion.
And yet...
The heart wants what the heart wants,
While praying to avoid a contusion.
And we soldier on flying a banner of hope
That our souls will find spiritual fusion.

<u>Random Thought</u>

You ever just get tired?
Even those who are at peace with the chaos
    around them get tired of being the strong
    ones.
The bigger person.
The voice of reason.
Those are the times when God's light in you
    shines the brightest.
You just have faith and endure and in Jesus'
    name, it shall all work for your good.

<u>Time and Space</u>

It is at twilights wax and wane that the reality
    of my solitude becomes prevalent.
The finite darkness is as a lover's embrace,
    and I receive it willingly.
Although, my mind remembers the warmth
    of the past and longs for reconciliation,
I am haunted by images of love's silhouette
    illuminated from antiquity.
Beautiful and elusive.

Declaration

Before I lay me down to sleep,
I'll write the words my heart doth speak.
If happiness is all I seek,
Why does this creature elude me?
Such simple a thing to want in life.
And a willingness to pay the price.
I feel like it's supposed to be mine
But the pursuit of it is my only right.

<u>Stay Strong</u>

I linger long
Listening to songs
Sung by creatures of the night.
And battle with my head
As it fills with dread
And thoughts of doom and fright.
Soon the night will grow cold
And I pray not my soul
As I hold on to twilight's flame.
Tomorrow's promise of change
Is uncertain and restrained
But hope and prayers will be maintained.

<u>My Romantic Mood</u>

I am in the mood to stimulate the cerebral
    erogenous zones.
Creating an explosion of orgasmic energy in
    the neocortex without one touch of hand.
Only the caress of words.
Are you ready?
(In my Barry White voice)
When was the last time your significant other
    took time to just breathe?
To walk up to you closely,
Gently pressing cheek to cheek.
You can feel their breath on your earlobe.
Anticipation for the touch of warm flesh
    causes goosebumps.
And they pull away.
Slowly tracing the line of your neck.
Hovering just above a touch to your
    shoulders.
Words being spoken through soundless
    rapture and received as the promise of
    Spring after a Winter chill.
Finally, a touch.
Caressing your face as their lips begin the
    journey of quenching your fevered thirst.
"Stop!"
"Don't move."
"Not yet."
The only words spoken...
When was the last time your significant other
    took their time?

LADIES AND GENTLEMEN, we have reached the end of this undertaking. This has been an amazing project for me. Not only has it been an opportunity for you to get to know a little about me, a total stranger, but I've also gotten to learn a few things about myself. I have been honest with you through every keystroke. The poems are mine. The stories are real, and the feelings are true. I hope that you have enjoyed my works. My final story...

A BEAUTIFUL YOUNG lady whom I attended high school with wrote me a poem once. I was, at that time, in a teenage version of "in love" with her. The title of the poem was "The Dreamer." It's strange to hear the words to that poem in my head tonight. Now although it was written as a rejection letter, I've always viewed it as a spotlight into my flawed emotional depts. I still remember it word for word. Not because of pain or scarring. It didn't do that. It's because that was the first time someone cleaned the mirror for me. Allowing me a true look at myself.

WE GROW, change, mature, and adapt but at your core, you never lose who you are. Life just builds around it. For all I've become and accomplished in my life I am still "The Dream-er." Hopelessly so. War-torn, battle-scarred, and in need of new armor but untainted... ME.

THE END.

LEAVE A REVIEW

Like this book?
Reviews are appreciated and welcomed. They can be as long
or as short as you'd like. Even star ratings are wonderful.
Thank you!

ABOUT THE AUTHOR

 Herbert McCants is a freshman book writer from Mobile, Alabama. At an early age he developed a love for words through music. His interest in poetry sprang from moving around a lot and always feeling like the odd duck amongst his peers.

As time passed his poetry took on a sort of self medicating, soothing voice of inward calm. As a man of 6'4" and an athletic build he spent a lot of time doing part-time work as a bouncer, DJ, and Club Manager, turning situations and real life events into springboards of writing material.

Soon the pull of the night life gave way to his need for spiritual growth. As his life changed so too has his writing. He's waiting on you at table 3, a cup of Caramel Macchiato Cappuccino in hand.

Email: atlashm64@yahoo.com

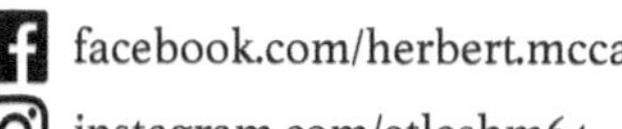
facebook.com/herbert.mccants
instagram.com/atlashm64